JUST A
CARDBOARD
BOX?

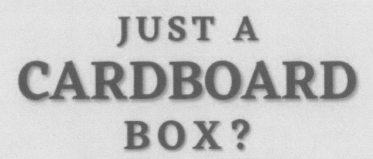

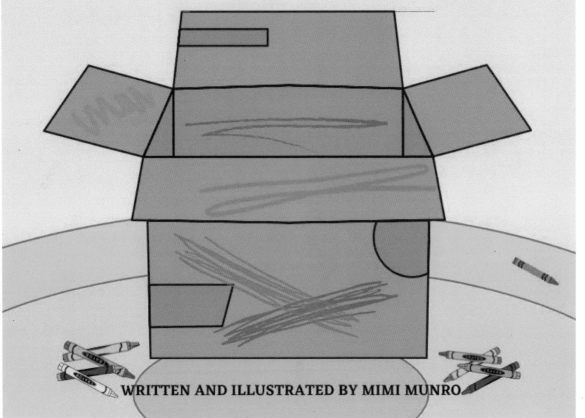

WRITTEN AND ILLUSTRATED BY MIMI MUNRO

THIS BOOK

BELONGS TO

....

"CAN WE KEEP THE BOXES, PLEASE?"

I ASKED THE DAY THEY CAME,

"THEY LOOK LIKE SO MUCH FUN TO ME,

I'D LOVE TO PLAY A GAME."

"HOW COULD THIS BE FUN?" SAID MUM

"IT'S JUST A CARDBOARD BOX."

"IT'S SO MUCH MORE THAN THAT" I SAID,

THESE ARE MY BUILDING BLOCKS"

"I COULD BUILD A CASTLE

AND TEDDY COULD STAND GUARD.

I COULD BE A MIGHTY MONARCH,

I BET THAT ISN'T HARD!"

"OOH, HOW ABOUT A RACE CAR?

I COULD EVEN MAKE A TRACK!

THEN DRIVE MY CAR AT SUPER SPEED,

FROM HERE TO THE COUCH AND BACK"

"OR I COULD MAKE A ROCKET SHIP,

FLY JUST LIKE A BALLOON.

ALL THE WAY UP THROUGH THE SKY,

TO A BOUNCY PILLOW MOON."

"I COULD EVEN BUILD A STEAM TRAIN

TO RIDE ON WITH MY TOYS.

ALL AROUND THE LIVING ROOM

AS I MAKE THAT CHOO CHOO NOISE"

'THEN WE'LL SET SAIL IN OUR PIRATE SHIP

AND HUNT FOR CHESTS OF GOLD.

AHOY! TO SOFA ISLAND

WHERE IT'S NEVER EVER COLD."

"I COULD BE A SUPER HERO

IN A COSTUME MADE BY HAND,

AND WITH MY SUPER POWERS

STOP AN EVIL ROBOT'S PLANS."

"I COULD FLY UP IN A JET PLANE,

MY TOYS A CHEERING CROWD.

WATCH MY TRICKS AND LOOPY LOOPS,

AS I WEAVE THROUGH PILLOW CLOUDS."

"I COULD EVEN BE A ROBOT,

JUST LIKE MY ROBOT TOYS.

I COULD GO TO ROBOT SCHOOL,

THAT'S A SCHOOL THAT I'D ENJOY."

"I COULD OPEN UP A TOY SHOP

AND BE A TOY SHOP KEEPER.

WHEN DINO WANTS TO BUY SOME BLOCKS

I'LL ZAP THEM WITH MY BEEPER."

"I COULD BE A WISE OLD WIZARD

AND WEAR A WIZARD'S HAT

I'LL WAVE AROUND MY MAGIC WAND

AND CAST A SPELL UPON THE CAT."

"I COULD MAKE A PUPPET STAGE

AND PUPPETS FROM ODD SOCKS.

I'LL DO A REALLY FUNNY SHOW

AND EVERYONE WILL WATCH."

"I COULD BUILD A GREAT BIG TOWER,

THE TALLEST ONE IN TOWN.

THEN WILL THROW BALLS AT IT

UNTIL I KNOCK IT DOWN."

"I CAN MAKE A SLIDE OF CARDBOARD,

FROM THE SOFA TO THE FLOOR.

IT CAN BE A SPEEDY RACE TRACK

FOR MY TOY CARS TO SOAR."

"WHEN IT'S ALMOST BEDTIME

WE'LL BRING SOME PLANTS INSIDE.

CREATE A COSY JUNGLE TENT

WHERE ME AND TED CAN HIDE."

"WHEN I FINISH PLAYING,

I'LL FOLD THE BOXES DOWN.

READY FOR RECYCLING,

WHEN THE BIN VAN COMES TO TOWN."

DID YOU KNOW A CARDBOARD BOX CAN BE
PLAYED WITH FOR HOURS AND HOURS?
IT COULD BECOME A MILLION THINGS,
EVEN GIVE YOU MAGIC POWERS.

COME READ THIS BOOK AND YOU WILL FEEL
THE MAGIC TAKE A HOLD,
OF YOUR IMAGINATION
AS THE GAMES AND FUN UNFOLD.

THIS IS THE FIRST OF MANY BOOKS
BY MIMI MUNRO.
TO KEEP UP TO DATE WITH NEW RELEASES,
PLEASE FOLLOW @MIMIMUNROSTORIES
ON TWITTER AND/OR INSTAGRAM.

Printed in Great Britain
by Amazon

87877251R00022